DESMOND COLE
GHOST PATROL

MERMAID YOU LOOK

by Andres Miedoso
illustrated by Victor Rivas

LITTLE SIMON

New York   London   Toronto   Sydney   New Delhi

LITTLE SIMON

An imprint of Simon & Schuster Children's Publishing Division
1230 Avenue of the Americas, New York, New York 10020
First Little Simon paperback edition July 2022
Copyright © 2022 by Simon & Schuster, Inc.
Also available in a Little Simon hardcover edition.
All rights reserved, including the right of reproduction in whole or in part in any form.
LITTLE SIMON is a registered trademark of Simon & Schuster, Inc.,
and associated colophon is a trademark of Simon & Schuster, Inc.
For information about special discounts for bulk purchases, please contact
Simon & Schuster Special Sales at 1-866-506-1949 or business@simonandschuster.com.
The Simon & Schuster Speakers Bureau can bring authors to your live event. For more information
or to book an event contact the Simon & Schuster Speakers Bureau at 1-866-248-3049 or
visit our website at www.simonspeakers.com.
Designed by Steve Scott
Manufactured in the United States of America 0622 MTN
2 4 6 8 10 9 7 5 3 1
Library of Congress Cataloging-in-Publication Data
Names: Miedoso, Andres, author. | Rivas, Victor, illustrator.
Title: Mermaid you look / by Andres Miedoso ; illustrations by Victor Rivas.
Description: First Little Simon paperback edition. | New York : Little Simon, 2022. |
Series: Desmond Cole ghost patrol ; 16 | Audience: Ages 5–9. | Summary:
Desmond and Andres visit the aquarium where they discover a mermaid whose song
puts anyone who hears it under a spell.
Identifiers: LCCN 2021054001 (print) | LCCN 2021054002 (ebook) | ISBN 9781665914086
(paperback) | ISBN 9781665914093 (hardcover) | ISBN 9781665914109 (ebook)
Subjects: CYAC: Mermaids—Fiction. | African Americans—Fiction. |
Hispanic Americans—Fiction. | Classification: LCC PZ7.1.M518 Me 2022 (print) |
LCC PZ7.1.M518 (ebook) | DDC [Fic]—dc23
LC record available at https://lccn.loc.gov/2021054001
LC ebook record available at https://lccn.loc.gov/2021054002

CONTENTS

CHAPTER ONE

UNDER THE SEA

It was HOT!

And when it was hot, there was really only one place to go. The pool!

Only, it was *so* hot even the Kersville swimming pool was boiling! *That's* how hot it was!

Ouch!

You know it's hot when kids dream about taking a trip to Antarctica just to cool off.

Not me, though. I know better. My parents went there once on a top secret science mission, and they had to bundle up so much that they could hardly move. And they were *still* freezing!

Count me out.

A girl on my block tried to escape the heat by building an ice fort inside her house, and for a little while it was the coolest place in Kersville. She'd figured out how to beat the heat!

Well, until the heat fought back . . . *and won!*

Just when we thought there was no way we could escape the scorching sun, we remembered Kersville had the perfect place to go: the aquarium!

The aquarium had *everything*! It had ice-blasting air-conditioning that turned kids into icebergs. It had shade so dark that it felt like being at the bottom of the ocean, as far

away from the sun as you could get.

Oh, and best of all, the aquarium had the coolest fish in the world. It was like an underwater zoo. And you didn't have to get wet to see them!

Plus, all those weird water creatures were behind glass, so you never had to worry about them getting you.

There were wriggly
octopuses, clownfish
as creepy as real clowns,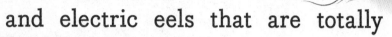
and electric eels that are totally
shocking! Oh,
and jellyfish
that sting,
cranky seals

with evil mustaches, and piranhas
that bite!

All of them locked
away behind glass.
How great was that?!

Some tanks had tiny fish that
zip around. Some had bigger fish

that stare at you like they're up to something . . . probably planning their escape. Hmmm, you should stay away from those fish. Especially the sharks.

Seriously.

However, if you're a kid who needs to touch the fish (YUCK!), the aquarium had a fish petting station (double YUCK!) just for you.

Me? No way. If fish were meant to be petted, they wouldn't live underwater, now, would they?

There *was* one time I touched a fish. It did not go well.

See, that's me, Andres Miedoso, running with a sea star stuck to my head and a waddling bird chasing me. And the kid with the other sea

star on his head? That's my best friend, Desmond Cole.

Oh, and the scaly thing riding the wave with all her fishy friends . . . that's a very angry mermaid.

Yeah, you heard that right. *A mermaid!*

DESMOND COLE

ANDRES MIEDOSO

9

Maybe I should have told you this before—Kersville isn't your typical town. Let's just say, it's *different*!

The mermaid used to be a secret, but it's safe to say that she's not a secret anymore!

But I'm getting ahead of myself. If you want to know what happened on that hot, hot day, let's start at the beginning, before everything started.

CHAPTER TWO

MERMAIDS AREN'T REAL

Don't let that chapter title fool you. Mermaids *are* real.

But on that Saturday morning, I didn't know that yet. Nobody did.

See, my parents decided to take me and Desmond to the one and only Kersville Aquarium.

It was way too hot to play outside, but that didn't stop us from trying. First, we tried a water balloon fight. 打架 That would cool us off, right?

Wrong. The water balloons burst into dust! **POOF!**

Then we tried playing in the sprinklers. That would be fun, right?

Wrong again. The sprinklers just sprayed us with hot air!

We even thought about playing on the slippy slide, but it melted on the grass into a gloppy mush.

So we all hopped into the car and headed for the aquarium.

I was excited, but not as excited as Desmond.

"What's everybody looking forward to seeing?" he asked on the way. "I can't wait to see the penguins!"

"No penguins!" Mom and Dad said at the same time, and they both looked afraid.

I wasn't sure why, but maybe it had something to do with their trip to Antarctica.

Mom changed the subject. "I want to see something I've never seen before . . . like a mermaid!"

"Sorry, Mrs. Miedoso. Mermaids aren't real," Desmond replied quickly. "They're just make-believe."

My jaw dropped. I'd never heard Desmond say something like that. He knew a lot of the things people didn't believe in *were* real.

After all, he was the one who started the Ghost Patrol!

Since I moved to Kersville, we've dealt with everything from ghosts to vampires to werewolves to zombies, and even a scary I Scream Man!

Desmond and I had seen a bunch of things people didn't believe in.

So why was he so sure mermaids weren't real?

"Mermaids *could* be real," I said.

"Absolutely, Andres," Mom agreed. "Anything is possible if you believe in it."

"Uh-huh," Desmond said, and I noticed a suspicious look on his face all of a sudden. "What do *you* think, Mr. Miedoso? Do you believe in mermaids too?"

"I believe in whatever Andres's mother believes in," he said, laughing.

"Well, there's one way to find out if they're real," I said, pointing out the window to the huge Kersville Aquarium sign. "We're here!"

If I'd known what was waiting for us inside the aquarium, I would have asked my parents to turn around and never look back!

CHAPTER THREE

O-FISH-AL BUSINESS

Stepping inside the aquarium was like stepping into the ocean. Everything was deep blue and green. And cold. Very, very cold! It felt so good!

While we stood in the long line to buy tickets, Desmond and I soaked up all that cool air-conditioning.

"Do you hear that?" I asked Desmond. There was a soft song drifting through the air. It was like the music was there and not there at the same time. It was hard to explain.

漂移

解释

Desmond nodded. "Yeah. I wonder where it's coming from."

The music didn't have any words. It was more like a hum, but it was catchy. I couldn't help humming along as we moved through the ticket line. Pretty soon, Desmond was humming too.

Hmm, hmmm, hmm, hmmm.

When we reached the front of the line, my parents handed over their credit card to buy tickets and— **WHAM!** We were surrounded by security guards and people in white lab coats.

"Mr. and Mrs. Miedoso," one of the lab coats began. "We need your *services* immediately."

Mom nodded.

"We're happy to help," she said. "Can our boys come with us?"

"I'm afraid not," a guard said firmly. "This is official business."

I had heard that before. This wasn't the first time my parents had to use their *services* to help solve a problem.

"You go ahead, Mom and Dad," I told them. "Desmond and I will be fine."

"Thanks, *mi hijo*," Dad said.

He tousled my hair, and then they left with the guards and lab coats.

Other kids might worry if something like that happened, but not me. My parents are top secret scientists, so I was used to it. I just hoped *the problem* had nothing to do with penguins. That would be bad!

"Are you ready?" Desmond asked me. "I think we should go see the jellyfish first."

And that's exactly where we headed.

CHAPTER FOUR

JELLYFISH DANCE

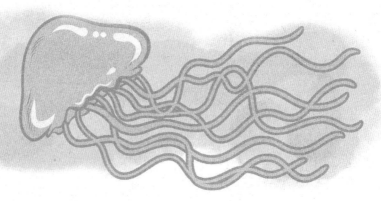

Desmond Cole has no fear.

I'm serious.

The first thing he did when we got to the jellyfish exhibit was put his face right up against the glass.

"Whoa, Andres," he said. "You need to check this out!"

I was standing just about as far away as I could get and still be in the same room.

"I'm okay over here," I called.

I didn't need to be that close to see the jellyfish anyway.

There were tall jellyfish, short jellyfish, wide jellyfish, and even upside-down jellyfish.

But no matter what they looked like, I knew all jellyfish had stingers. 刺

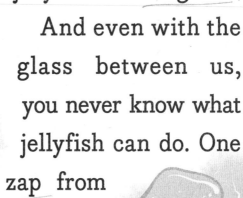

And even with the glass between us, you never know what jellyfish can do. One zap from those scary-looking stingers, and you were down for the count!

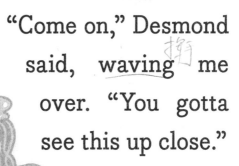

"Come on," Desmond said, waving 揮 me over. "You gotta see this up close."

I watched as plenty of other kids, even little babies, pressed their faces close to the glass. I sighed. Maybe it wasn't so dangerous. And the jellyfish did look kind of cool, sort of like little aliens in the water.

So I inched closer to the tank to see them better, and—wow! A school of purple jellyfish glided right by me.

It was magical.

All their stinger things wiggled like streamers at a big surprise party. I was hypnotized.

That was when I heard that song again . . . the humming. And I wasn't the only one. The grown-up next to me started humming along.

"Do you hear that too?" I asked her. But the grown-up ignored me and kept on humming.

Huh? Sometimes grown-ups were weird. But so were jellyfish. I looked at them again, and *they were dancing to the music.*

Then all the people in the room were dancing too—just like jellyfish! Even Desmond!

Everyone was swaying around with their arms dangling and swinging in the air. It was wild!

Next the jellyfish stopped moving, and it actually looked like they were watching the people dance. The humming got louder and louder and louder.

That was when I saw a pair of glowing eyes in the water, hidden behind the jellyfish.

And the eyes were watching *me*!

If you know me, you'd know that in situations like this, the first thing I'd do is shriek a note so high it would have broken all the glass in the aquarium.

But this time, some kind of power had come over me. Instead of screaming and running away, I began to walk even closer to the jellyfish tank. Closer and closer until . . . **BONK!**

I hit my head on the glass.

And just like that, the spell was broken and all I heard was . . . a lot of laughing.

Laughing *at me*!

"Be careful, Andres!" Desmond chuckled. "Just because you can see through glass doesn't mean you can *walk* through it too."

The other people in the room kept laughing. It was so humiliating.

"Come on," Desmond said. "Let's go check out the sharks next."

I looked at the tank again, but now the eyes were gone. Or maybe they were just hidden behind the jellyfish again. I couldn't be sure.

Then again, maybe I hadn't really seen eyes to begin with. Maybe I'd just imagined them.

CHAPTER FIVE

SHARK PARK

I'd never been so happy to see sharks in my whole life.

I mean, it's not that I like sharks. In fact, usually I steer clear of them. But after the jellyfish room, and feeling those creepy eyes on me, sharks weren't nearly as scary.

"Welcome to the Shark Park," Desmond said.

"They should call it the *Too Dark Shark Park*," I mumbled.

I could hardly see anything in the room. Most of the light was coming from inside the huge shark tank that surrounded the whole space, giving off a dark blue glow.

Pretty soon, the room filled up with kids oohing and aahing as the sharks swam all around, like they were watching us. They reminded me of my parents when we go grocery shopping—wandering up and down the aisles looking for something good to eat!

The kids didn't care, though. They stayed close to the glass, but all the parents sat on benches, looking at their cell phones. The lights from all those phones made the room brighter, which was kind of annoying.

Why do parents need to be on their phones all the time?

I turned back to look at the sharks with extremely sharp teeth as they swam in front of us. They really were something! We saw a hammerhead shark, a tiger shark, and one I called Jaws because it yawned right in front of us. Its mouth was enormous!

But the lights from all those cell phones behind us got brighter and brighter. Then the phones started beeping!

"Are parents playing games on their phones?" Desmond asked.

I shrugged. I didn't know what they were doing.

But I knew one thing: The sharks were wondering what was going on too. They all moved toward the glass, really close to us kids.

"Hello, pretty shark," said a girl
standing next to me.

And when I looked over to see who
she was talking to, I wished I hadn't.

The shark's nose was pressed up
against the glass, but it wasn't looking
at the little girl. It was looking at *me*!

Gulp.

As a matter of fact, all the sharks started looking at the kids like they were mad. I wondered if the glass would hold a team of angry sharks.

"Hey!" Desmond shouted to the parents. "Turn off your phones! The light is confusing the sharks. They don't like it!"

But the parents didn't listen to him. Why? Because they were too focused on their phones. That's why!

Desmond was right. With all those lights on, the sharks were acting meaner and hungrier. They were looking at us like we were dinner. I thought I actually saw one of the sharks lick its lips!

We needed the Shark Park to get dark again. But how? Desmond was about to jump into action when that song started.

Hmm, hmmm, hmm, hmmm.

And you know what? The humming seemed to calm the sharks down. They stopped glaring at us and began swimming happily around their tank again. And then something happened that *really* surprised me.

The parents put away their cell phones!

Grown-ups almost never put away their phones, especially when they're focused on something they say is *important*.

With all the phones gone and the lights turned off, it took us a few moments to adjust to the darkness again.

And when we did, Desmond and I saw something else we'd never seen before: There was a person inside the tank . . . *with* the sharks!

CHAPTER SIX

BIRD ALERT

Desmond and I screamed at the person in the tank. "Get out of there! You are surrounded by sharks!"

We were about to bang on the glass when we heard someone else say, "STOP!"

A guard stepped in front of us.

"No tapping or BANGING on the glass allowed," he said. "We don't want to disturb the sea life."

"But someone is in there!" we told him.

"A person in the tank with the sharks? Impossible!" the guard said. "Sometimes we send a diver down

to clean the tank, but we move the sharks out of there first. Maybe your eyes are playing tricks on you."

"See for yourself," Desmond said.

We all peered into the shark tank but . . . whoever we had seen was gone!

Talk about strange!

The guard shook his head at us and walked away.

"Okay, guess what I'm thinking," Desmond whispered to me.

"Are you thinking there's something *fishy* going on here?" I asked with a smile on my face.

"Ha! That's a good one!" Desmond said, laughing. "But no. I'm just thinking we should go get some food. Those hungry sharks reminded me we haven't eaten anything."

Wow! Desmond *always* thought about food!

"Besides," he said, "you should never solve a mystery on an empty stomach."

True. So true.

So we left the Shark Park and

walked over to the snack bar. There
were so many yummy treats to
choose from, but both Desmond and
I wanted the same thing: the Super
Ocean-Salted Orca Pretzel.

I'd heard about that pretzel. Some kids called it "The One That Got Away" because it was so big and so salty that no one had ever finished it by themselves. Good thing Desmond and I were going to share it.

A minute later, we were totally munching on that pretzel. And wow, it was soft and warm and *so* salty. Desmond and I weren't even talking. We were just eating.

Suddenly, there was a flutter of wings beside me. Then I heard a croak that sounded kind of like a pig and kind of like a frog.

"What was that?!" I asked.

My mouth was full of pretzel, and my heart was full of fear.

Before Desmond could answer, we heard a grown-up at the next table say, "Look, kids. It's Bessie!" Then his kids clapped and clapped like trained seals. 拍手

"What's a Bessie?" I asked the man.

"Bessie is the pelican who lives at the aquarium," he explained, pointing to the bird. "It's feeding time now. Go ahead."

That was when his kids started throwing scraps of their food to Bessie, but they missed, and the scraps landed on me!

And I guess Bessie was really hungry . . . because she started eating me!

I have to be honest, being pecked by a pelican tickled at first. But then things got weirder because the humming started again. Only this time, it was much louder.

All the parents and the kids around us just froze. The only ones who were unfrozen were me and Desmond. And Bessie.

SQUAWK!

Bessie started flapping her wings wildly as the humming got louder and louder. Then she flew right at us.

We dropped our pretzel for her, but she didn't go for that.

She was after *us*!

Desmond and I raced across the aquarium, past a bunch of people, but nobody helped us. They were too busy looking at the fish.

We kept running and running. When we turned a corner, we spotted a wall of fish, and it actually looked like they were waving us over . . . with their tails.

But that couldn't be, could it?

Desmond and I stopped running and walked closer to the fish.

That's when they all scattered to reveal the glowing eyes I'd seen before.

My heart started racing. My mouth dropped open.

And Bessie the pelican bit me on the butt.

CHAPTER SEVEN

MERMAID YOU LOOK

"Yee-OUCH!" I screamed.

Okay, okay. Bessie didn't bite me. It was more like a nibble, and it didn't really hurt. But it definitely surprised me.

Desmond was surprised too. But not about Bessie.

He was staring at the aquarium, where swimming right in front of us was an actual, real-life . . . mermaid!

The mermaid had big glowing eyes, a fish tail, and long hair that floated all around her like seaweed. And the water in the tank seemed to ripple and dance to the same music everyone was hearing.

The song was coming from the mermaid!

"I know what you're doing," Desmond said to the mermaid. "Mermaids can enchant people with their singing."

"Wait, what?" I asked him. "What does that mean?"

"It means they can put you in a trance and get you to do whatever they want," Desmond explained.

"But you said mermaids weren't real," I reminded him. "So how do you know all this stuff about them?"

Desmond smiled slyly. "Because a mermaid will never show themselves if you believe in them."

And that's when it clicked into place for me. Desmond had been on a mermaid hunt all along, which was really cool.

But the mermaid had been on a Desmond and Andres hunt, which was definitely *not* cool!

How do I know the mermaid was after us? Well, because she bellowed, "Capture them!"

At first, Desmond and I stood there frozen as all the fish swam over to the window. We weren't too worried about them because they couldn't do anything to us from behind the glass. As a matter of fact, I laughed.

"You're going to have to try harder than that to get to us!" I snapped.

"Uh, Andres," Desmond said, pointing behind me.

When I turned around, I saw a group of grown-ups and kids walking toward us. They were under the mermaid's spell! 中魔

"I think it's time to run," Desmond whispered to me.

And when Desmond Cole tells you to run, you better run!

CHAPTER EIGHT

DO NOT ENTER

Have you ever been chased by an angry mob of people and sea creatures? Honestly, I would not recommend it.

Here's the reason: When you're in an aquarium, there's nowhere to hide.

Correction: There's nowhere to hide from the fish.

Because they are everywhere, and they point you out to all those people under the mermaid's spell.

For real, the fish formed giant arrows pointing to us, the jellyfish were glowing around us, and even the electric eels made glowing-lighted signs that spelled out THEY'RE HERE!

And don't forget about Bessie. Yep,
she was still after us too!

Desmond and I ran and ran until we
found a door that said DO NOT ENTER.

So naturally, we entered.

I mean, normally, I try to follow signs, but not when I'm being chased by a mob of people under the spell of an angry mermaid. Sometimes you have to break the rules!

The door led to a back room that was filled with fish tanks and people in lab coats. Oh, and my mom and dad were there.

And they were standing next to a mersurfer.

"Mom? Dad? Mersurfer?" I began. I really didn't know what was going on.

"Andres? Desmond?" my mom asked. She sounded just as confused as I did. "Mersurfer? What's a mersurfer?"

"I am, dude," said the mersurfer. "That's what I've been trying to tell you all day."

Then he turned to me and Desmond.

"S'up, beach bruhs?" he asked. "Can you lay some knowledge on these scientist peeps?"

What could I say? How could I tell my parents about the time we met mersurfers on the beach? And how could I tell them about the mermaid?

Parents can't handle stuff like that!

Before I could decide what to do, the mermaid's humming song drifted into the room.

Two seconds later, my parents were under the mermaid's spell. And so were all the other people in lab coats.

We were trapped.

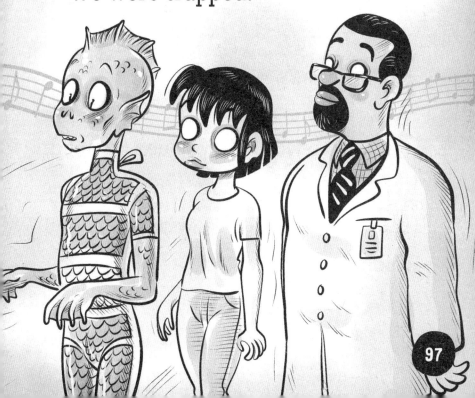

Well, we would have been trapped. But here's the thing: You're never trapped when you're with Desmond Cole.

He knew exactly what to do.

Desmond released a penguin from one of the fish tanks, and it waddled over to my parents.

My mom shrieked. My dad howled.

And that's how we knew the spell was broken.

"Get it away from me!" my mom screamed, tossing the penguin to my dad.

"I don't want it near me!" my dad yelled, tossing it back to my mom.

Back and forth they went until the penguin landed safely in the arms of the mersurfer.

"I've got you, little dude!" the mersurfer said.

The good news: All the wild action seemed to break the spell for everyone in the room long enough for me and Desmond to escape.

The bad news: We didn't escape the aquarium like I was hoping. We were headed right toward the fish petting station.

CHAPTER NINE

A GAME OF CATFISH AND MERMAID

"Follow me! I've got a plan," Desmond said.

I should have known he would have a plan. Desmond *always* has a plan!

When we got to the fish petting station, Desmond said, "Time to set a trap for the mermaid."

"How?" I asked. "She's in the water behind the glass."

"Not for long," Desmond said. "First, we're going to block the doors so people can't get in here. The only way in will be through the water system. That's how they get the sea life in here."

"And that's how the mermaid will get in," I added, finally figuring it out.

"Yes!" said Desmond, nodding. "And when she gets in here, we'll use this giant net to catch her. The end!"

I had questions. Of course I did. Like where was Desmond keeping that giant net this whole time? And why would catching the mermaid end things?

I mean, what were we supposed to do with a mermaid in a giant net?

But there was no time to ask any questions. Sometimes you just had to trust Desmond Cole.

So we put the plan into motion. We blocked the doors, and Desmond set up the net. Then we waited and waited.

And waited.

"Maybe there's something stuck in the waterway," I suggested. And I tugged at the net to make sure it wasn't blocking anything.

That's when a gush of water burst through. I mean A LOT of water!

A sea star smacked me right in the face and clamped on tight. I jumped back so quickly that I crashed into Desmond, and we both splashed into the water!

You can probably guess what happened next, right?

The mermaid burst through on a
wave with all the fish!

And so did Bessie the bird, who
was squawking up a storm.

We were surrounded!

And as water filled the room, it looked like Desmond and I were all washed up.

Well, until our mersurfer buddy swam by, that is.

He waved to the mermaid and said, "Whoa, Melody. Be chill to my little buds, Andres and Desmond. They are *way* cool dudes."

Desmond and I looked at each other. It was the first time we had ever been called way cool dudes. And I liked it!

CHAPTER TEN

MELODY

It turns out that Melody the mermaid and the mersurfer were old friends from the ocean, long before Melody moved to the Kersville Aquarium.

It also turns out that Melody loves living at the aquarium.

She adores watching all the kids who come to visit.

And even though it looked like she'd wanted to make Desmond and me swim with the fishes, she just wanted to make sure we kept her secret a secret.

And okay, yeah, I just told *you* her secret now, but let's keep that between us, okay?

"Kids love the aquarium, and the fish love kids," Melody said with a smile on her mermaid face. "But when grown-ups started bringing their phones in, they stopped paying attention to what's really important."

"The fish?" Desmond asked.

"No, the kids!" Melody replied. "Grown-ups forget how wonderful the world can be, but kids never forget that. That's why I sing my song. It reminds grown-ups of what it feels like to be a kid again. My song even makes them put away their phones and spend time with their kids, looking at all the beautiful fish."

Melody's song had a lot of power. I wondered if it was strong enough to help my parents stop being scared of penguins? Nah, *that* would never happen!

But the next time you're at an aquarium, listen for a magical song. Maybe ask your grown-up to listen for it too. The fish can hear it, even those scary old sharks.

That's because every aquarium in the world has its very own mermaid, and if you hear the mermaid's song, it might just make you *sea* the world in a whole new way.